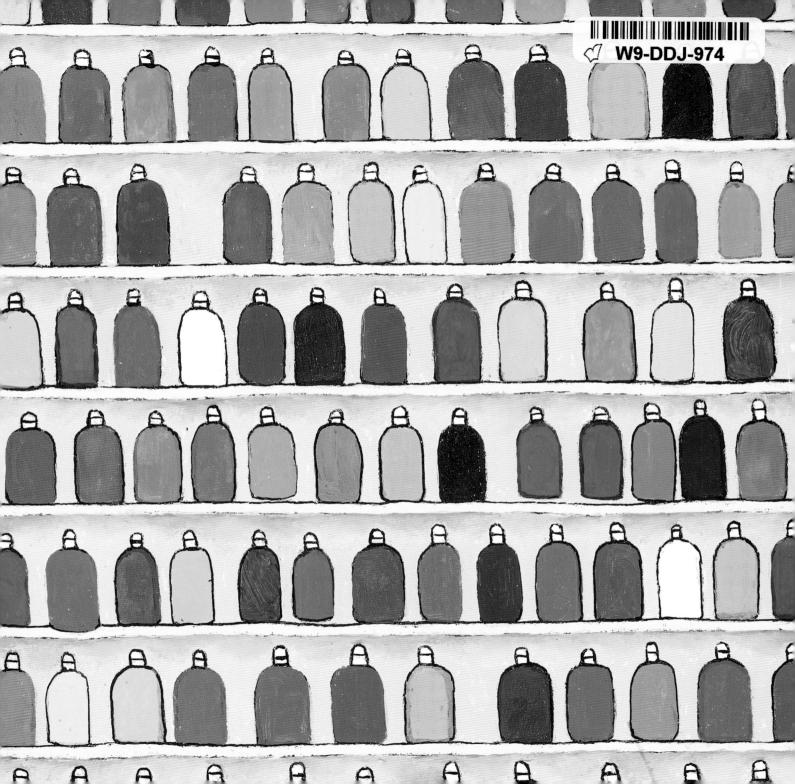

the surprise

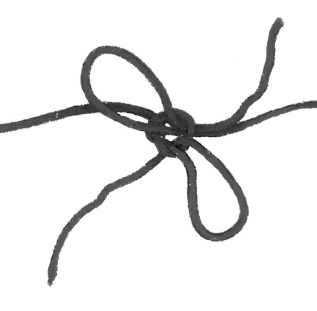

Library of Congress Cataloging-in-Publication Data

Ommen, Sylvia van.
   [Verrassing. English]
   The surprise / Sylvia van Ommen.
      p. cm.
   Summary: In this wordless picture book, Sheep goes to great
lengths to surprise Giraffe with a lovely red sweater.
   ISBN-13: 978-1-932425-85-7 (hardcover : alk. paper)
   [1. Sheep—Fiction. 2. Giraffe—Fiction. 3. Stories without words.]
   I. Title.
   PZ7.W519648Su 2007
   [E]—dc22
                              2006018296

LEMNISCAAT
An Imprint of Boyds Mills Press, Inc.
815 Church Street
Honesdale, Pennsylvania 18431

Sylvia van Ommen

the surprise

LEMNISCAAT
Asheville, North Carolina

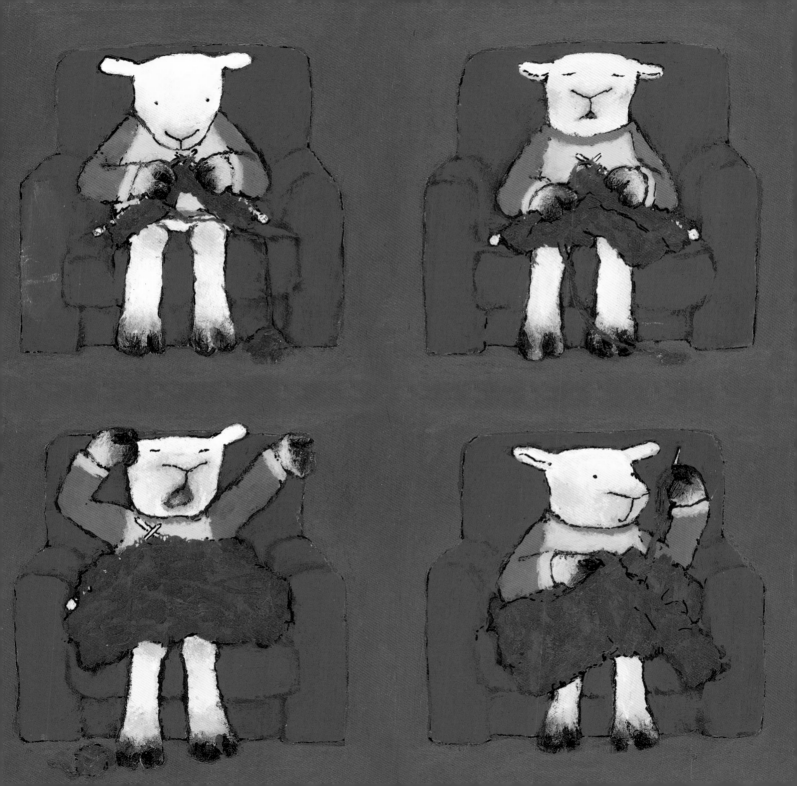

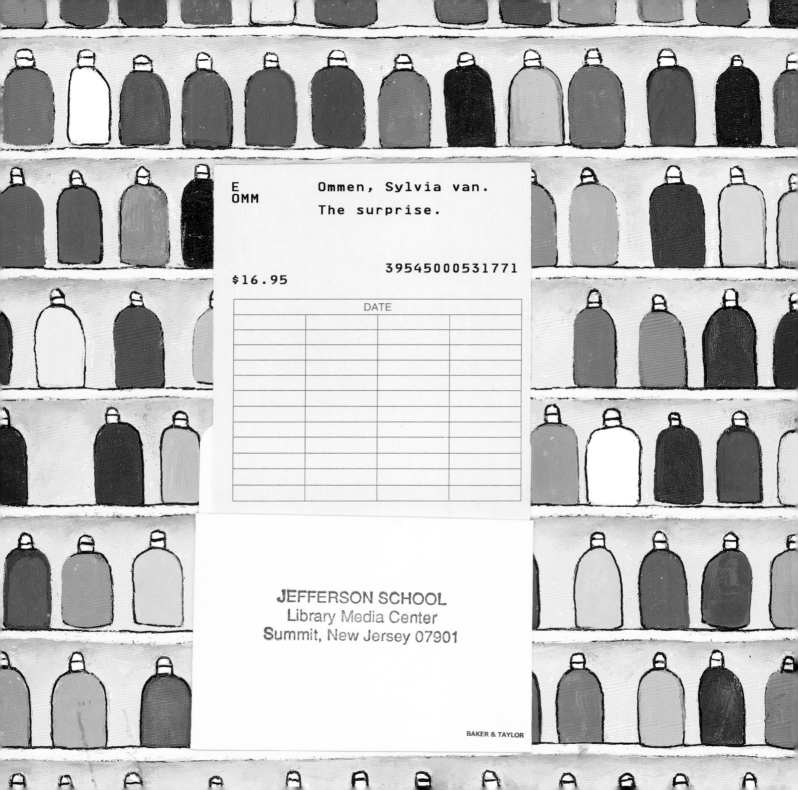

E
OMM   Ommen, Sylvia van.
             The surprise.

                              39545000531771
$16.95